Richard is a qualified instructor and has been teaching adults and children to ski since 2007.

He started skiing in 1987, whilst at school, and from the moment he put on his first pair of skis, he was hooked.

Richard became a BASI Alpine Level 1 ski instructor in 2007 and then continued with the UK Advanced qualification in 2011.

He enjoys spending time with his family and loves hill walking, mountain biking, photography and, of course, skiing in his spare time.

This is his first adventure into the world of publishing!

High above the villages there are little creatures that live in the mountains called marmots.

You'd be very lucky to see one, as they live underground. But if you listen carefully, you can sometimes hear them whistle to each other.

In the summer they love to play in the long grass and during the winter they hide away in their cosy burrows beneath the snow.

However, there is one little marmot that loves to come out and play all winter, and his name is Monty!

Monty the Marmot loves exploring the mountains and before he goes out to play he enjoys a big bowl of warm porridge oats.

Monty loves the snow and is very good at skiing.

“I am off to see my new friend Mortimer”, he said to his mummy.

“Make sure you wrap up warm, the snow is deep today and it’s cold outside”, she replied.

Mortimer was on his first ski holiday and staying with his family in the village.

“Hi”, said Monty as he met him at the chalet door. “Are you coming out to play?”

“Yeah! What can we do today?” he asked.

“Shall we go up the mountain? We can ski down and see my friends Holly and Elin”.

“Ski?” replied Mortimer, “But I don’t know how to ski?”

Oh dear thought Monty, and he tried to think of other things you could do in the snow if you didn't ski…

"I'm an instructor, I'll teach you!" he then said.

"Wowzers!" yelled Mortimer, "I've always wanted to ski".

"Brill!" Monty replied, "We need to get all the gear before we start… follow me". And with that Monty led his friend off to Big D's Big Ski Shop.

“Hi Guys!” greeted the huge shop owner.

Monty and Mortimer said hello and asked what they would need for the lesson.

“To start with, you’ll need lots of warm clothes, gloves and big socks. Then you’ll need these”, and he handed Mortimer a pair of skis.

“You’ll also need a helmet, just in case you fall over”, said Big D.

“Which you will”, giggled Monty.

Then he gave him a pair of ski boots. “Wowzers! They’re super heavy”, said Mortimer as he tried them on.

BIG DS SKI SH
HE HE!
1000 SKI FACTS
SKI INFO

Outside the shop, Holly and Elin flew past at great speed. "Hi! Looks like you are having fun!" Monty shouted to them.

"Yeah, we're off for hot chocolate at Mrs Bear's Cake Cabin".

"Wowzers! Are we going up there?" Mortimer asked while pointing back up the mountain.

"No silly, not yet", said Monty.

They both stepped into the bindings. **Clunk! Clunk!** And before he knew it, Mortimer was standing with a ski on each foot!

"Can you feel how slippy the snow is?" asked Monty.

"Yeah! Coolio smoolio!" he laughed.

HEY!
WOW!

Monty showed him the ski map and then they went over to the lifts where Roy was waiting to help.

"Stand still!" said Roy as Mortimer stood on the moving magic carpet.

"Coolio!" he said as he looked at the view from the top of the lift.

"Everyone in ski school starts on this green slope first", said Monty.

"Green?" Mortimer looked puzzled. "The snow isn't green, it's white?"

Monty laughed, "The slopes are named after different colours", and Mortimer remembered the wiggly lines on the map.

"The green runs are easiest", said Monty, "And the hardest ones are black. Those are my favourite!"

Mortimer looked down the slope. He was very excited and couldn't wait to have a go.

"Hey! What shape are my skis making on the snow?" Monty asked as he started skiing.

Mortimer looked at Monty's skis. It was difficult to see but he could just make it out from how Monty was standing.

He then tried to think of things the same shape and realised it was like a slice of pizza!

"It's a snowplough", said Monty. "Make sure you don't let the front of the skis get tangled up".

Then it was time for Mortimer to have a go. "Coolio-io-ioo!" he yelled as he started to slide down the hill.

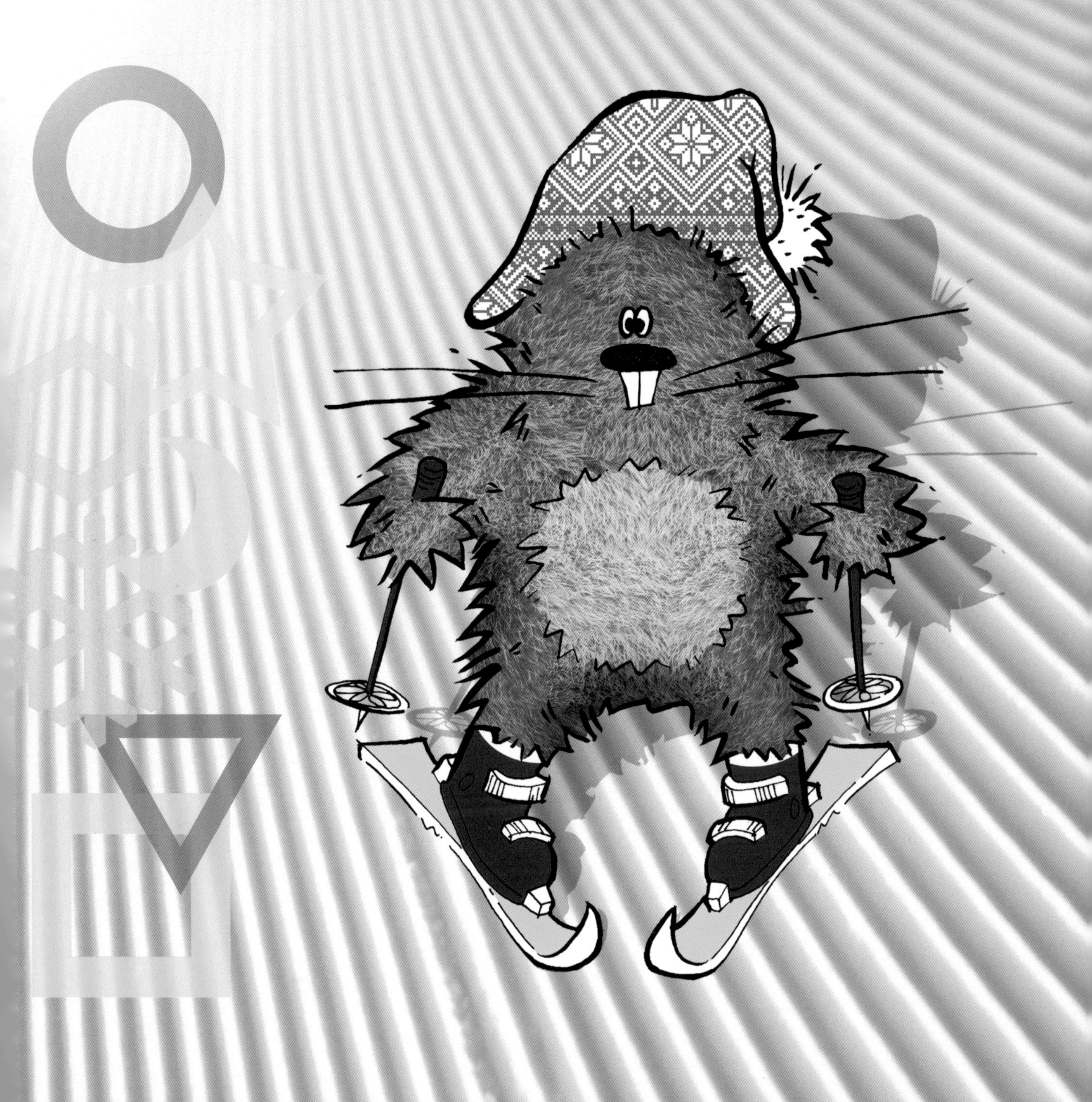

Monty watched as his friend snowploughed towards him. “Well done! The bigger the snowplough, the slower you will go.”

“Or the bigger the slice of pizza, the slower you go!” He giggled back.

“Okay, let’s keep practising”, said Monty. “But don’t lean back or you might fall over”.

But Mortimer forgot to snowplough and started to gather speed. His skis were now straight and no longer looked like a slice of pizza. He went faster… and faster… and faster until...

Monty couldn’t watch, then all of a sudden there was a huge…

YIPEEEEEE!!
UH OH!

CRASH!

Mortimer went flying into a huge pile of soft snow at the bottom of the slope. **Oops!**

But he was okay and Big D helped him get up on his feet again.

"Phew!" Mortimer yelped.

"Try again" said Monty. "And this time keep it slow". So Mortimer put his skis back on and had another go.

"That's it", shouted Monty. "You're skiing!"

CRASH!

EEEK!

OH!

WHARRRRR!!

So that was it, Monty had taught his friend how to ski and they practised for the rest of the day.

"You've done really well and earned your first Marmot Ski Award!"

"Brill, can we go again tomorrow?" asked Mortimer.

"Yeah, for sure!" Monty replied.

It was now snowing a little and they were both getting very hungry and very tired.

Roy stopped his lift and packed his things up. It was time to for them all to go home for tea and cake.

The snow continued to fall on the mountains, the lights came on in the villages and the groomers came out to prepare the pistes for the next day.

Mortimer was so excited about what they had done, and all he could think about was what exciting adventures the next day would bring.

He told his family all about it and then went off to bed to dream about his new favourite hobby…

SEE YOU NEXT TIME!

The Marmot Ski Awards...

LEVEL 1

You can use a snowplough (pizza slice) shape to ski down a gentle slope and stop.

LEVEL 2

You can do snowplough turns on a gentle slope.

LEVEL 3

You can do turns on a steeper slope and use the lifts without help.

LEVEL 4

Top Skier! You can ski in control all over the mountain.

...what level are you?

This book has been written and illustrated to help inform and develop young skiers. The terminology used is designed to introduce the world of skiing to children who are learning to ski or going on their first winter holiday.

This book does not replace the need for real instruction from a qualified ski instuctor.

All the images are digital collages from original photographs; and drawing pen on detail paper.

The text is set in Garamond and Thug.

ISBN 978-0-9926675-0-4
First Printing, 2013
Printed in the U.K.

Published by Ski Bat Publications

montythemarmot.co.uk